mister corbett's ghost

Other books by Leon Garfield

THE GHOST DOWNSTAIRS
GUILT AND GINGERBREAD
JACK HOLBORN
JOHN DIAMOND
THE DECEMBER ROSE

mister corbett's ghost

Leon Garfield

Illustrated by Antony Maitland

Viking Kestrel

To Nancy and Edward

VIKING KESTREL
Penguin Books Ltd, Harmondsworth, Middlesex, England
Viking Penguin Inc., 40 West 23rd Street, New York, New York 10010, U.S.A.
Penguin Books Australia Ltd, Ringwood, Victoria, Australia
Penguin Books Canada Limited, 2801 John Street, Markham, Ontario, Canada L3R 1B4
Penguin Books (N.Z.) Ltd, 182–190 Wairau Road, Auckland 10, New Zealand

First published 1969 in *Mister Corbett's Ghost and Other Stories*
This edition published 1982
Reprinted 1987

Text copyright © 1968, 1969 by Leon Garfield
Illustrations copyright © 1982 by Antony Maitland

British Library Cataloguing in Publication Data available

Library of Congress Catalog Card Number: 87–50173

ISBN 0-670-81652-3

Printed in Great Britain by
Butler & Tanner Ltd, Frome and London

1 A windy night and the old year dying of an ague. Good
riddance! A bad old year, with a mean spring, a poor
summer, a bitter autumn—and now this cold, shivering
ague. No one was sorry to see it go. Even the clouds,
all in black, seemed hurrying to its burial somewhere past
Hampstead.

In the apothecary's shop in Gospel Oak, the boy Partridge
looked up through the window to a moon that stared fitfully
back through the reflections of big bellied flasks, beakers and
retorts. Very soon now he'd be off to his friends and his home
to drink and cheer the death of the old year – and pray that the
new one would be better. And maybe to slip in a prayer for his
master, Mister Corbett, the apothecary himself. Such a prayer!

'May you be like this year that's gone, sir, and take the same shivering ague! For your seasons weren't no better.'

He stared at the oak bench that shone with his sweat – and at the great stone mortar and pestle in which his spirit had been ground.

'May you creak and groan like your shop sign in this wild wind, sir.'

Now there passed by in the moon-striped street a pair of draper's apprentices. Friends. They grinned and waved as they went, and their lips made: 'See you later, Ben!'

He waved back. They glanced at one another, looked up and down the street, and then came leaping quaintly to the shop where they fattened their noses on the window, making pinkish flowers in the glass.

Benjamin made a face. They made two, very diabolical.

'Can we come in, Ben?'

'Yes – for a moment.'

Into the strange and gloomy shop they came, with looks of cautious wickedness.

'Make a brew, Ben.'

'Make a bubbling charm.'

'Turn old Corbett into a rat or a mouse . . .'

Like the forced-up sons of witches, they had begun to caper round the great stone mortar. Glumly, Benjamin looked on, wishing he could oblige them, but not knowing how.

Huge wild shadows leaped among the retorts and crucibles, but they were the only uncanny things about . . . save in the apprentices' minds. Now they began to screech and laugh and caper more crazily than ever, so that their faces seemed to dance in the heavy air like rosy fire-flies.

'Turn him into a worm!'

'Turn him into a snail!'

'Turn old Corbett into a beetle, Ben – and step on him!'

'Be quiet!' cried Benjamin of a sudden. 'He'll hear!'

The draper's apprentices grew still. The stairs at the back of the shop creaked. But then, so did every other mortal thing in that blustering night.

'Turn him into a – '

But Benjamin Partridge did not hear what other witchcraft was being asked of him. His mind was suddenly distracted: partly by listening to a further creaking of the stairs, and partly by a chill and a darkness – like a cloud across the moon – that passed over his heart. He shivered. His two friends stared at him: then to each other. They shrugged their shoulders.

'Happy New Year, Ben.'

Then they left him for the more cheerful street. With their going, the chill within him grew curiously sharper. His back itched, as if he was being watched. He went to the window and waved his friends on their way; and in the jars that sat like short fat magistrates on the shelves, no more than a tiny waving Partridge was reflected. A drab-dressed little soul of a boy seemed to struggle to get out.

Now it was half after seven o'clock. Time to be gone. He pulled his patched grey coat from under the counter and began to put it on.

'Sharp to be off, Master Partridge?'

Slippered Mister Corbett was slunk down his stairs, quiet as a waistcoated rat. Or had he been on the stairs all the time? Uneasily, Benjamin wondered what his master had heard. Mister Corbett's lips were pressed tight together. A muscle in his cheek twitched and jumped; his hands were clenched so fiercely that the blood was fled from his knuckles as if in dismay. Could he have heard?

'It – it's half after seven, Mister Corbett, sir.'

'What's half after seven when there's work to be done?'

His unpleasant eyes, swollen by spectacles, stared round the shop. 'There's dust on the bottle-tops, Master Partridge. Would you leave it so? Polish the bottles before you go.'

The apprentice sighed, but did as he was told. And Mister Corbett, pale of face and round of shoulder, watched him.

'Not willingly done, Master Partridge. Too anxious to be out and wild as a fox.'

'It's twenty to eight, Mister Corbett, sir. It's New Year's Eve – '

'What's New Year's Eve when there's work to be done?
There's a smear of grease on the bench.'

Once more the apprentice sighed, but polished away at the
mark that had been left by his own sweat.

'Not willingly done, Master Partridge. Your heart wasn't in
it. Still less was your soul. I want your heart and soul, Master
Partridge. I expect them. I demand them.'

His eyes grew hard as he spoke and blotches came into his
grey cheeks. He saw his apprentice was defiant, and would keep
his heart and soul for himself.

'It's five to eight, Mister Corbett, sir. I would be home – '

'What's your home to me, Master Partridge? What's your
family and friends to me when I've not got your heart and soul?
For you're no use to me if I don't have all of you. There's a
dribble of wet on that flask by your hand, Master Partridge.
Wipe it off.'

The wetness was a fresh-fallen tear, but the apprentice
scorned to say so – even though others were beginning to leak
out of his bitter eyes. Eight o'clock and his friends would be
waiting and his mother would be laying up a fine table . . .

The apothecary peered once more round his shop. Was there
nothing else to be done? Momentarily, his eyes flickered towards his private doorway behind which dwelt his wife and
children in his private world.

The boy watched him hopefully, fancied he'd glimpsed a
softening . . .

'Then – ' he began; but there came an urgent tapping at the
window. The apothecary smiled harshly.

'A customer, Master Partridge. How lucky you're still here.
Open the door for the gentleman. And wait.'

A retired lawyer's clerk, maybe – or a neglected scrivener.
Very small and old and dusty, and all in black. Very wrinkled
about the cheeks – as if he'd put on a skin the cat had slept on.
He brought a queer smell into the shop with him, damp and
heavy: an undertaker, perhaps?

Mister Corbett rubbed his hands together and showed all his
teeth in a dreadful smile.

'Not shut? Still at work, eh?' muttered the old man sniffily, as if he had the beginnings of a chill.

Benjamin Partridge eyed him miserably. An old fellow like him would need a deal of medicine. And then to what purpose?

'Never too late to be of service, sir,' said the apothecary. 'Me and the apprentice. Heart and soul in our trade. No matter what the time – or the day. Heart and soul, eh, Master Partridge?'

The old man nodded briefly and seemed not to notice the furious dismay in the apprentice's face.

'This mixture, then. Very important. Want it tonight. Can you oblige?'

He gave the apothecary a paper. Mister Corbett read it. He frowned. He glanced round his shelves. Then he smiled again. (What ugly teeth he had! Like railings.)

'Pleased to oblige, sir. Will you wait?'

The old man sniffed very hard. By chance, it seemed, his curiously bright eyes caught those of the apprentice. But once more he appeared not to notice the wretchedness in them.

'Wait? On New Year's Eve? And in my state of age and health? No. Deliver it. I'll be in Jack Straw's Castle. Not too far, eh? He – he! Deliver it man. And soon.'

With that he was gone – remarkably quick and spry for a man in his state of health – and leaving behind in the shop an unmistakable smell of graveyards.

The boy Partridge shut the door after him but was too angry and distressed to notice that he'd vanished from the street, though no sound of horse or carriage had been heard.

Back in the shop, the apothecary had begun on measuring and weighing and grinding and mixing, and his apprentice looked on with ever-mounting misery and dismay. New Year's Eve was ticking slowly and surely away.

At last it was done. The mixture was bottled and ready. Hurriedly, Benjamin cleaned and cleared away till the shop shone like a new knife.

'Was it willingly done, Master Partridge?'

'Willingly – willingly!' cried Benjamin desperately.

His coat was on again. He was at the door. It was half after nine, and he had a long walk home. In his wild need to be out and away he turned pleadingly to his master.

'They'll be waiting now, sir! I must be gone! Everything is clean and shining. Nothing's left undone. A - a happy New Year to you, sir!'

'Yes, indeed, Master Partridge,' smiled Mister Corbett. 'You're willing enough. So a happy New Year to you - '

Benjamin was in the street. His face was shining, his hopes were suddenly high again. In an hour he'd be home -

'But of course you'll deliver this mixture first, Master Partridge?'

Mister Corbett's hand held out the bottle, and Mister Corbett's eyes stared cruelly into his. Benjamin's heart turned to lead. Had it been in the apothecary's hand at that moment, even he, with all his chemical knowledge, would have pronounced it to be lead.

'B-but it's all of three mile, sir! Three dark and windy miles! It'll be the New Year afore I'm back! They're waiting on me - '

'If they love you heart and soul, Master Partridge, they'll keep on waiting - '

'But there's thieves and footpads and murderers - '

'Pooh!' declared the apothecary generously. 'What will such fellows want with a lad in a patched coat? Safe as a coach and four, Master Partridge! Believe me, poor clothes give better protection than chain mail.'

'But there's gibbets and corpses and, most likely, ghosts - '

'Then take you this extra jar, Master Partridge,' beamed the apothecary, handing him such an item, 'and if you should be lucky enough to meet with a spectre, phantom or ghost, then snip off a piece of it and bottle it quick. Then you and I will examine it shrewdly - and send it off to Apothecaries' Hall! Ha-ha!'

'But - but - ' stammered Benjamin, despairing of anything else to move his master. For some strange reason, he could not come out with what troubled and disturbed him almost as much as his loss of New Year's Eve.

'But – but – ' he struggled, and still could not say what was creeping coldly round his heart. The old man: the uncanny customer in black, who repelled him in the queerest way.

Thieves and gibbets and murderers were one thing. The dusty old man who had smelled of the grave was quite another. For when he'd come, there had passed once more, like a cloud across the moon, a darkness and a chill over Benjamin's heart. He shivered in his cracked boots.

'But – but what if I lose my way, sir?' he came out with at length.

'What's this?' cried the apothecary angrily, for he'd lost patience, standing out in the cold. 'Did you think *I'd* go, then? Or did you think I'd send Mrs Corbett or one of my own children? Is *that* what's been fermenting in your unwilling mind, Master Partridge?'

Wretchedly, Benjamin shook his head.

'Won't you – take pity on me, sir? On this night of all nights?'

Harshly, the apothecary stared down at his white-faced apprentice. Maybe too much chemistry had turned him to iron.

'Pity, Master Partridge? What's pity when there's work to be done? Be off with you! And if you should weary on the way, remember – it *may* be a matter of life and death. Run fast, Master Partridge. Run as if – as if *my* life depended on it!'

2 'So I'm to run as if *your* life depended on it, am I,
Mister Corbett? Well – well, watch me, then! You
just watch me as I nip up this hill.

'Lord, Mister Corbett! Was that a snail that passed
me by? For shame! Who'd have thought a snail would have
beaten an apprentice running as if his master's life depended on
it?'

Benjamin Partridge shook his head as if surprised to discover
how leadenly he was mounting up dark Highgate Hill.

'Dreadful thing! Imagine old Mister Corbett perishing in
Gospel Oak. Breathing his last.

'But here comes Benjamin, a-pounding through the winter's
night! See that bush ahead? If I reach it before I can count to
ten, Mister Corbett'll be saved! Hurry – hurry!

'*Eleven!* Just too late. And after I tried! Heart and soul, Mister Corbett. Just as you'd have liked . . .'

Benjamin Partridge, now near the top of Highgate Hill, fixed his young face into a crooked smile. He'd a strong imagination and saw – in his mind's eye – the apothecary corpsed and coffined in his neat back parlour (the holy place!) with a wreath at his feet inscribed:

FROM BENJAMIN PARTRIDGE. IN RESPECTFUL MEMORY.

Then, from a distance, a clock struck ten and the apprentice listened in dismay. Such chance as he'd had of reaching his home before New Year was now almost gone.

He wavered. Looked behind him – then ahead. A curious frown flickered across his face, and he began to hurry – even to run; yet not without mumbling into his wretchedly thin coat that he was making no haste on Mister Corbett's account and that he'd sooner yield up his heart and soul to the Devil than leave them in pawn in Gospel Oak.

A coachman turning into the Gatehouse Tavern out of the creaking night, was much struck by the hurrying boy's face – which passed him patchily and then was gone on, into the cheerless dark.

'Such a mixture of anger and dismay as had no business hanging about chops so tender and young. But God send him a happy New Year, and spare him from some of this bitter wind!'

The night was now grown wilder and the wind banged and roared about the air like an invisible tiger, madly fancying his stripes to be bars. (Pray to God he don't get out!)

'Rot you, Mister Corbett! May this wind blow you to Kingdom Come! May it whistle through your skin and play its tunes on your mean old bones!'

On and on he ran (but not for Mister Corbett's sake!), now stumbling, now turning this way and that to avoid the wild passion of the night. It seemed to be striving to pluck him off the world by his coat tails, did that queer and even extraordinary wind that blew mainly from Islington, Wapping and Tower Hill.

Seven churches with open belfries stood direct in the wind's path from Wapping: St Bride's, St Jude's, St Mary's, St Peter's, St Michael's and St Michael-on-the-Hill's. Through each of them it flew, making the black bells shift and shudder and sound unnatural hours. The very ghosts of chimes and the phantoms of departed hours. Twenty-eight o'clock gone and never to return. What a knell for the dying year!

Benjamin Partridge put his head down into his skimpy collar and hastened on faster yet. (But not as Mister Corbett would have had him hasten. There was a darkness in his spirit quite out of the apothecary's chemistry.)

His right-hand pocket was bulky with the bottle for the queer old customer, and his left hand banged against his knee, reminding him of Mister Corbett's little joke – the empty jar for 'the piece of a ghost'.

'A piece of you, Mister Corbett – that's what I'd like in your jar! And I'd set it on me mantelshelf at home, as neatly labelled as you'd like. Apothecary's heart. Very small. Very hard. Very difficult to find.'

Now the wind came wilder yet, and it seemed – to the buffeted boy – to have a strange smell upon its breath. It smelled fishy and riverish (as became its Wapping origins) and sweetish in a penetrating kind of way.

The Lord knew where it had been or what unsavoury heads it had blown through! Heads of chained pirates drowned under three tides at Shadwell Stair, full of watery fury; heads of smiling traitors, spiked on the Tower, full of double hate; heads of lurking murderers in Lamb's Conduit Fields, heads of lying attorneys, false witnesses, straw friends, iron enemies, foxes, spies and adders . . .

A sudden screaming from Caen Wood caused Benjamin Partridge to clap his hands to his ears and fairly fly. What had it been? A committee of owls over a dead starling? Most likely . . . most likely . . .

Ahead lay a little nest of lights winkling out the dark. The

Spaniards' Inn. Sounds of singing and laughter came faintly from within. A cheerful company, drinking out the dying year.

The turnpike keeper in his tiny house hard by saw the boy pause and stare towards the inn with miserable longing on his face.

'Poor devil!' he thought. 'To be out on such a night!'

Then he saw the boy shake his head violently and mouth the word 'No!' several times before hurrying on into the cheerless dark.

'God send you a happy New Year!' he murmured. 'And spare you from some of this bitter wind.'

Benjamin Partridge's head had suddenly been filled with dreams of another, more cheerful company, made up of his friends and his mother: candle-lit and fire-warmed faces to the window, waiting on his coming.

Then the wind had blown out these dreams and left nothing but darkness within him.

There seemed to come over his hastening form a curious difference. His running was grown more purposeful. At times, he seemed to outpace the wind itself – bending low and rushing with an oddly formidable air. His coat tails flapped blackly, like the wings of a bird of ill omen.

'Coming for you, Mister Corbett. Coming for you!'

Already he could see the top of Hampstead Hill. On either side of him the trees bent and pointed, and high upstairs the tattered clouds flew all in the same direction. The dark wind was going to Hampstead, too, and it was in the devil of a hurry.

At last, he could see Jack Straw's Castle: a square-built, glum and lonely inn scarce half a mile ahead. Doubtless, the queer customer was sat by the parlour fire, snuffling for his mixture. Then let him snuffle till the cows came mooing home! Benjamin Partridge was on a different errand now.

He continued for maybe another thirty yards. Then he stopped. To his left lay a path, leading down into the dark of the Heath.

A curious darkness. Earlier, there had been rain and certain roots and growths had caught a phosphorescence; spots of light glimmered in the bushy nothingness.

Before, these uneasy glintings might have frightened the boy, for they were very like eyes – and malignant ones at that. But now he scarcely saw them: the dreadful wind had blown out of his head all thoughts but hatred for the mean and pale apothecary who'd sent him forth.

He began to descend the path. The earth was wet and sobbed under his feet.

'May you sob likewise, Mister Corbett – when I'm done with you!'

For the first part of its length the path dropped pretty sharply, and soon Benjamin was out of the worst of the wind. But in its place was a wretched dampness that crept and clung about him. Likewise, there was a continual breathing rustling that seemed to inhabit the various darknesses that lay about the path.

Several times he paused, as if debating whether or not to abandon his purpose and fly back to the high road and on to the inn. This path was disquieting, and it was growing worse. But each time he seemed to see Mister Corbett's face before him, mouthing, 'Heart and soul, Master Partridge. I want 'em.' And Benjamin Partridge went on: for hatred, though it may harden the heart, softens the brain, renders it insensible to danger, and leads it in the way of darkness, madness and evil ... At the end of this terrible path, there stood a terrible house.

It was a tall, even a genteel house, often glimpsed from the high road from where it looked like a huge undertaker, discreetly waiting among the trees.

What was then so terrible about it that even the whispering darkness, the crooked trees and the crooked sky were small things beside it? The visitors it had.

Old gentlemen with ulcers of the soul for which there was no remedy but – revenge! Ruined gamblers, discredited attorneys, deceivers and leavers, treacherous soldiers, discharged hangmen, venomous servants, murderous constables ... coming chiefly at dusk, furtively grinning for – revenge. In this grim regiment Benjamin Partridge now numbered himself.

The path grew level. One by one the glinting eyes winked shut as shrubs obscured them.

'And so may your eyes shut, Mister Corbett: just like that! Ah!'

Benjamin Partridge stopped. Before him stood the house. Three pairs of windows it had, but they were dark. An iron lantern swung in the porch making queer grunting sounds as it swung against its hook. *Ugh ... ugh ... ugh....* But the three candles within burned untroubled.

There was a lion's head knocker on the door. A good brass knocker such as might have cost five pound in the shop by Aldgate Forge. (Or had it been cast in a deeper forge than Aldgate, even?)

The boy shivered ... most likely from the damp. He knocked on the door. A harsh and desolate sound. Came a flap of footsteps: very quick. Then they stopped.

The boy made as if to draw back – maybe to make off, even at this late stage? *No.* He knocked again.

'Nails in your coffin, Mister Corbett.'

The door opened. The boy cried out. Candle in hand, peering out with unnaturally bright eyes, was the queer customer! He said: 'I thought you'd call here first – '

3 It was said there was a room at the top of the house where certain transactions took place. The windows of this room were sometimes pointed out, for they could be seen from the high road, staring coldly through the trees.

It was rumoured that this room, ordinary enough in all its furnishings, held an item so disagreeable that it chilled the soul. Visitors had been known to stare at it, lose their tongues, fidget, then leave in haste never to return.

Benjamin peered past the old man into the dark of the house. His eyes glanced upward. Catching this look, the old man dropped his gaze in an oddly embarrassed fashion.

'Are you – are you sure, young man?'

(Was there truly such a room? Or was it all a tale told by apprentices at dead of night?)

The old man sniffed.

'Forgive me, young man – but are you sure? I must know. We don't want to waste our time do we? You've considered? You've thought? If you change your mind now, I won't be offended. Far from it! In a way, I'll be pleased. There, young man! I see you bite your lip. So why not turn about and forget it all? I'll not say anything. All will be forgot. We've never met! Come, young man – that's what you really want, ain't it? It was all a foolish idea – the black thought of a black moment. So say no more and be gone!'

He paused and stared at his young caller with a quaintly earnest air. He took a pace down so that he and the boy stood on a level. They were of a height. Maybe, even, Benjamin was a shade taller.

'Admit now – your heart and soul ain't in it?'

An unlucky expression! Whatever of doubt or uneasiness Benjamin might have felt (and he felt both, for he was but human) shrank beside the sudden image of skinny, grinning Mister Corbett grating, 'Heart and soul, Master Partridge. I want them. I demand them!'

'Let me in,' muttered Benjamin bleakly.

The house smelled of graveyards – as did the old man – but otherwise it was no glummer than the parlour in Bow. The old man shrugged his shoulders, as if he'd done what he could, and led the way.

'This way, young man. Tread carefully. The stairs are treacherous. I don't want your death on my hands!'

So there was such a room aloft.

Benjamin's heart began to struggle in his breast. His breath came quickly and made thin patterns in the candle light. The old man paused. He jerked the candle down, thereby causing banisters and certain respectable pieces of mahogany furniture to take fright and crouch in their own shadows.

'Remember, young man – it's heart and soul or nothing!'

Again, fear and doubt fell away as Mister Corbett's face was before Benjamin. His heart grew steady under a ballast of two years' hating.

'It's heart and soul, all right! And I'll tell you – '

'Tell me nothing!' interrupted the old man curtly. 'No reasons, *if* you please! Reasons ain't my concern. Had my fill of 'em, young man. Reasons that would freeze the ears off a brass monkey. Payment's my concern.'

Nervously Benjamin felt in his pocket. Not much there. But he hoped with all his heart and soul it was enough to procure – Mister Corbett's death!

'Nothing now,' said the old man, observing Benjamin's action and divining its result. 'I don't aim to beggar you. My terms is fairer than that. A quarter of your earnings from now till – '

'Till when?'

'Till you die, young man. Just till then. And then you're free. Paid up. Discharged. Now, no haggling *if* you please. This ain't a market-place. Take my terms or leave 'em. A quarter of everything from now till Doomsday. I always deal in quarters. Always have and always will. So it'll be fivepence out of every one and eight pence. Or, if you prosper (and please God you do!), five shillings out of every pound. No more: no less. Don't be offended, young man. I always put my terms straight. Ask anyone . . .'

But Benjamin was not disposed to ask anyone. The terms seemed reasonably fair, future payment being a cheerfuller prospect than present expense. He nodded in as businesslike a fashion as the circumstances allowed.

The old man shook his head and, with many a painful sigh, continued upward into the night.

'Another floor, young man. The top of the house.'

'I know,' said Benjamin.

Again the old man paused. He peered down over the banister with an air of resentment, as if a confidence had been betrayed and a secret blown to the winds. He seemed to shiver before mounting the remaining stairs briskly. Benjamin followed.

'This is the room,' said the old man, and pushed open a door.

For no reason but expectation, Benjamin shrank back into his pitiful coat. Yet the room was quiet. A fire burned subtly in the grate, and the furnishings were as genteel as everything else in the house. True, there was a smell of graveyards, but no worse than in the hall downstairs.

'Come inside,' said the old man, lighting a second candle. 'Come in and sit you down.'

His voice had grown suddenly courteous, as if long custom in that room had got the better of him. 'Take a chair by the fire, dear sir.'

But Benjamin did not hear him. He was peering round for the dreadful item that was to chill him to the soul.

'The chair, sir. Take a seat. This is journey's end.'

Benjamin recollected himself, attempted to smile, then sat in a chair as ordinary as an attorney's. Likewise the desk the old man was fumbling in, and a sideboard that supported the candlesticks – all as ordinary as sin.

There was a painting above the mantel of a tragical woman in an old-fashioned blue dress. Most likely the old man's mother – else why was she there? And what could be more ordinary than that? No: there was nothing uncanny anywhere.

'Now, young man – your name, *if* you please?'

'Partridge. Benjamin Partridge.'

'And – and the *other* name?'

'Corbett. Apothecary Corbett of Gospel Oak.'

The old man wrote carefully, then sanded the paper and put it away in a drawer. While he was engaged, Benjamin peered round the room once more.

The wall facing the window was taken up with shelves. Shelves from floor to ceiling. Shelves about a foot apart and divided into pigeon-holes.

So the old man liked pigeon-holes? Nothing chilling in that. What did he keep in them? Impossible to see. Sharp shadows obscured each opening – save one. A gleam of white could be seen. Benjamin stared.

Lord! Was it – was it a *pudding bowl*? Yes indeed! And cracked. Benjamin all but grinned at the absurdity of it.

'Have you,' said the old man gently, 'anything about you that *he* has touched lately? Anything will do. Just so long as he's touched it and his warmth's been upon it.'

Benjamin started. The old man had left the desk and was standing before him, hand outstretched. Confusedly, he felt in his pockets and found the empty jar for the 'piece of a ghost'.

'Yes!' said the boy angrily. 'Here's something he touched! Rot him!'

'All in good time,' said the old man, and took the jar.

He examined it carefully . . . so carefully that his withered old lips seemed to touch it.

What now? He began to fish about in his pockets. (Lord, he must have been wearing as many coats as a hackney carriage driver!)

At last he found what he wanted. Nothing worse than a length of black ribbon.

Without another glance at the boy, he wound it round the neck of the jar and tied it in a curious knot. Then he took up a candle and shuffled over to the wall of shelves. As he drew near, he raised the candle so that by chance it illumined each and every pigeon-hole.

Now the boy's soul grew cold as ice. He shook and he shuddered. A chill crept through his veins.

In each of the pigeon-holes lay a singular item. An item of no great value. An item that bore no relation to its neighbour – save one thing.

Here, there was a pincushion; there, a pair of spectacles; beneath, was a silver fork; beside it, a lace handkerchief – and beside that, a child's doll, very fixed-looking. In one hole, there lay a pistol, and in another, a piece of wax candle . . .

Items as far apart as could be imagined, with but one odd, trifling thing in common. Each had tied about it, and fastened with a curious knot, a piece of black ribbon!

'It's done,' said the old man quietly. Mister Corbett's jar had joined its neighbours.

'Is he – he is . . . dead now?' whispered Benjamin, unable to tear his eyes from that wall of mortal hate.

'In minutes, young man. Nothing can save him now. No need to worry. If you leave directly, you'll see it. Come, young man – it's nearly time.'

But try as he might, Benjamin could not look away from the shelved wall. He'd seen a hat he thought he knew. The hat of a gentleman who had lived nearby – till he'd died last month: much beloved, universally mourned.

Who had brought that hat?

The old man sensed the boy's distress. He moved the candle away from the wall so that all the pigeon-holes sank back into their separate blacknesses.

'Everyone fancies they recognize an item there,' he murmured. 'But, believe me, it's most unlikely. It really is!'

He took the boy's arm. 'Now you must hurry. Back to the road, else you'll miss him. And that would never do! After all, it's the chief part of what you're paying for!'

His fingers were strong. They fumbled down to the boy's bone causing sharp pains to inhabit his arm from shoulder to finger-tips.

There were no more words between them. The old man snuffed the unnecessary candle and, holding the other, drew Benjamin from the room.

Where was the black-ribboned jar? On which shelf? Vainly, the boy glared over his shoulder as he was pulled from the room. All was darkness: his own offering not to be distinguished among dolls, spectacles and pudding bowls. Such an insignificant thing was his hatred!

Silently – save for the sound of his own rough breathing and the old man's snuffles – they went down the stairs and back to the front door.

Not so much as a: Goodnight, young man, did the old man utter; still less a: Happy New Year. Maybe he thought he'd already done enough in that direction?

All he said as they stood momentarily on the porch was: 'Remember, Benjamin Partridge of Gospel Oak, a quarter of your life's earnings. Monthly. My usual terms. Now, hurry or you'll miss it! His time's all but at full stretch!'

Did he then push the boy back on to the path? Or did Benjamin stumble? He fell face down and heard the door shut and the knocker tremble faintly.

He got to his feet. His fall, and now the general night damp, conspired to make him vilely cold. He pushed his hands into his pockets and found the old man's medicine – still undelivered.

He turned to go back. The porch light was doused. The house – more like a great undertaker than ever – was of a misty black. He shivered, and turned again towards the high road.

He'd been advised to hurry. So hurry he did: along the disquieting path that sobbed under his feet like a heart-broken child. . .

At last he reached the road. Thank God, the wind was much diminished. Overhead the clouds hung in vague, disturbing shapes – some horned, some winged, some with jaws agape.

There came a sound of running feet. He looked along the road towards Highgate. His heart quickened. He began to sweat.

Towards him, limping and panting, spectacles agleam in the moon (whose light did nothing but bad for his leprous complexion), came Mister Corbett!

Nearer and nearer he came. Was he grinning? How ugly were his teeth!

But what now? His bony hands reached out – as if he would clutch and speak. To say what? Nothing.

Even as he reached to touch the boy his face curdled, his eyes fell up and his mouth fell down in a long, black O.

The old man had done his business capably. Mister Corbett was dead. His body dropped down in the road. And over it stood Benjamin Partridge: revenged.

There was not so much of pleasure on the boy's face. He was not situated for it. Alone he stood, under the high night, beside the corpse of the master he'd wished dead with all his heart and soul.

'I didn't do it,' he whispered uneasily. 'I never touched him!'

4 'You asked for it, Mister Corbett! As the moon's my witness, you asked for it! One kind word out of you and I'd not have gone to the house. As this moon above is my witness!'

Benjamin Partridge turned from the corpse and peered at the moon: his witness.

His witness! Fearfully he stared up and along the road. Who else, beside the moon, had seen? No one. Not a living soul anywhere – save his own.

With difficulty, he smiled ... then caught Mister Corbett's eye. Disagreeably, the apothecary's spectacles still shone in the moonlight. Being lifeless, they'd failed to die.

'I'm off now, Mister Corbett. And there's nothing you can say that'll keep me this time!'

He began to walk, but soon stopped and looked back. There lay the corpse, face upward, silently shouting to the moon.

Benjamin swallowed, but there was no moisture in his throat. He attempted to walk again. A frightening thought struck him. What if he should meet with someone while the dead apothecary was still in sight? Would not that someone put two and two together and make an unfavourable four?

'Murderer!' they'd shout. 'Murderer! He's murdered his master! Catch him! Hang him!'

No doubt about it. With much circumspection he began to creep back.

Dear God! How them spectacles shone under the moon! Fair blazed, they did! Once more, he stood by the dead man. Best move him off the road. Best tumble him among the bushes. Blame the footpads. Blame the weather, even – but don't blame Benjamin! *He* never laid a finger on him.

Damn the old man! Why did he have to fetch Mister Corbett out on to the road to give up his dingy ghost? Why couldn't the perishing have been quiet and respectable in bed? Or even in the shop? Just dropped down behind the counter like an old broom?

'Rot you, Mister Corbett! You're as horrible dead as alive! But not for long!'

He bent down and seized hold of the apothecary's coat and pulled with all his might.

'You're a dead weight, Mister Corbett, skinny that you are! Your bones must be made of – of lead!'

The apothecary's head dropped down on to his chest, as if apologizing for the trouble he was giving his apprentice.

They were at the edge of the road. One more heave and Mister Corbett would be safely over it and rolling down into the spotted dark.

How queer the gleaming patches looked, for the phosphorescence caught off the earlier rain still persisted. Maybe it was even more remarkable than before: like a fine fall of stars.

No. More like eyes. Why, they seemed to be in pairs!

'One last heave and it's good-bye for ever, Mister Corbett!'

Benjamin made ready. Glanced once more along the road. Peace and quiet either way.

'Sleep well, Mister – '

The spots of light! They were shifting. Impossible! The circumstance was distracting him – unsettling his sight. And small wonder!

'Sleep well, Mist – '

They *were* moving! They were circling about. They were creeping nearer and nearer, and always in pairs. They *were* eyes!

The boy let go of his burden with a cry of dismay. The Heath was alive. Dark and obscure shapes were rising up from it. Shapes of ragged, powerful men. A dozen, fifteen – even twenty of them. Monstrous fellows who stared and grinned and scowled.

'Coming with us, young 'un?' murmured a voice. 'For it looks like that's where you belongs!'

'Done 'im in,' muttered another admiringly. 'Neat as kiss-your-'and. Needle, knife or skewer, young 'un? What did you use? My, but you're a nifty slicer!'

'I – I never touched him,' whispered Benjamin, half out of his mind with terror.

'We all know that one!' mumbled a third voice, fruity with phlegm. 'We've all tried that one – from time to time. "Never touched 'im, yer Honour. 'E just fell dead at me feet!" But they 'angs you just the same, young 'un.'

On which there was a confused sound of agreement and these violent, desolate creatures from the darkness began to climb up and over the edge of the road.

Very bushy they were about the chops, and thorny and horny in their skins. They were the lurking murderers and footpads of the Heath.

'Neat ... very neat indeed,' mumbled a foxy brute with a torn cheek. 'Get you five shilling a time for work like that anywheres. What say, young 'un? Make a tidy forchun between us. Never seed a man dropped so neat!'

'I never touched him,' moaned Benjamin: on which the

felons laughed silently, exposing their broken teeth to the moon.

'You'd best come along with us, young 'un,' repeated the first speaker. He was a tall, lean man with some rags of authority about him. Maybe a dismissed sergeant or the mate off some doubtful ship?

He made to lay his hand on Benjamin's shoulder, but the boy shrank back. The man stank to the stars.

'Not good enough for you, you little grey-faced rat? Giving yourself airs? You'll be sorry for that!'

Angrily he turned to his companions. 'Don't no one 'elp 'im. Though 'is back may break and 'is 'eart may crack, don't no one 'elp 'im. We ain't good enough for 'im. So let's be going, brothers.'

Now there followed a truly dismal sight. One by one, each of these grim men returned to the dark of the Heath and one by one came back, bearing a heavy burden. Drunken wayfarers, boozed horseboys who'd missed their way, servants who'd taken short cuts, even a youth who'd strayed to look for his hat the wind had blown away. Old men, young men, men who'd been in the prime of their lives, now lying like dull old bags across powerful shoulders – in the prime of their deaths. Murdered, each and every one.

But none so neatly as Mister Corbett.

'Makes you ashamed, don't it?' wheezed the foxy man, who grunted under a fat coachman he'd drowned in the Whitestone Pond.

'W-where are you going?' whispered Benjamin, whose terror, by this time, had passed all mortal bounds.

'To the Highgate graveyards,' replied the foxy one softly, as if anxious not to be heard talking to him. 'We always does. Can't leave our 'andiwork to rot and betray us, can we? We buries it, friend – good and deep.'

They were all upon the road again. The tall man, who wore his corpse like a bulky halter, nodded, and the melancholy procession began to shuffle along the road to Highgate.

'Best come along, young 'un – else you'll be took and 'anged.'

'But I never touched him!' moaned Benjamin piteously. 'They can't hang me for nothing!'

But who would believe him? In all truth, his situation was not promising. The abominable Mister Corbett gaped accusingly up at him. Plainly his chief hope lay with those who, from experience, knew best.

He bent down and seized Mister Corbett's chilly wrists. He pulled and heaved and strained. His back cracked, his heart nearly burst, but at last Mister Corbett was folded across his shoulder with a bony hip digging into Benjamin's neck.

It was monstrously uncomfortable, but nonetheless, with tottering steps he hastened on, striving to overtake the glum crew ahead.

Which was not difficult, for his horrible foxy friend with the fat, wet coachman loitered and complained of his lot.

'Catch me death,' he kept muttering. ''E's soaking through to me lungs. 'E must ave took up 'alf the pond inside of 'im. For that's what 'e's discharging now! Still – I saved 'is watch from a wetting, so it weren't for nothing. It's an ill wind, as they say! What did you prig from your'n, young 'un?'

Benjamin, who'd thieved nothing from Mister Corbett save his life, felt suddenly awkward and almost ashamed.

'How much farther?' he panted. 'He's growing that heavy!'

'Leastways, he ain't wet,' mumbled the drowner. 'Leastways, you'll not be catching your death! Be thankful you got a skill, young 'un, and can drop 'em neat. Make a forchun between us – if you should change your mind!'

Benjamin shook his head as best he could against the obstruction of the dead apothecary and shuddered. Not for the hugest fortune in the world would he have joined this dreadful procession nightly. All he longed for was to get Mister Corbett safely underground.

There was a halt ahead. Much shuffling and grunting and soft cursing as dead arms gently swung and smacked the backs that had borne them. Why the delay? Constables? God forbid! No: they were arrived at the toll-house.

Formidable legality: not to be avoided.

A copper oil lamp hung on a bracket outside the toll-house, lighting the list of tolls.

For a man and a horse . . . one penny halfpenny.
For a man, a horse and cart . . . fourpence halfpenny.
For a coach and four horses . . . one shilling and sixpence.
For cattle, sheep, pigs . . . two shillings the score or part thereof.
For a man and a corpse . . . seven shillings and sixpence.

Lord, but the turnpike keeper took a mean advantage! But in the circumstances, what could a poor murderer do? Pay up – or be hanged!

'Pay up or be hanged!' joked the keeper as the grim gentry crowded at the gate.

'Rogue!' 'Villain!' 'Lousy thief!' 'Stinking robber!' were the various greetings, spoke low and weary.

There came a general heaving as of a black mountainous sea, followed by the clink of coin as hands went to obstructed pockets and found the passage money.

One by one they paid up and passed on, till at last it was Benjamin's turn.

'Pay up or be hanged!' grinned the keeper, hand outstretched.

'Four shillings. That's all I've got,' mumbled Benjamin.

'Don't no one 'elp 'im!' called out the lean man sourly.

'Sorry, young 'un,' breathed the foxy gent. 'Can't afford new friends in our line of business. See you in hell, maybe.'

With that he turned his back and shuffled off into the dark towards the Highgate graveyards, with the drowned coachman weeping over his shoulder and seeming to wave a shrewd good-bye.

Very soon, they were gone – the creeping murderers – and even the creaking of their feet was lost in the ordinary sounds of the night . . .

'Pay up – or be hanged,' repeated the keeper.

'For God's sake, sir, won't you take my four shillings? I got to get through! Can't you see, I got to bury him?'

The keeper shook his crafty head.

'Sorry, lad. No exceptions, else where would we be? Letting
'em all through for sixpence in no time!'

'Then – then I'll leave him and be gone alone!' cried Benjamin in violent desperation.

'Oh, no you don't, lad! I want none of *your* rubbish left here!
Be off with you – *and* take your quiet friend! Lord, but he's an
ugly customer all right.'

'But I can't run no further! My back's breaking and my
heart's on the burst! Take pity on me!'

'Sorry, lad. There's no room for pity in our line of business.
You must take your chances with your ugly friend; and I fancy
they ain't so good.' He cocked his head on a far-off sound.
'Don't want to depress you, lad, but there's a coach on its way.
And coming quick. Yes, lad, I'm a-fancying your time's come.
And all for the want of another three and sixpence.'

'But I never touched him! I never touched him!'

On which the keeper laughed, then laughed louder yet, for
the lumbered apprentice had begun to run . . .

Dear God in heaven, what a piece of running it was. All the
devils in hell must have screamed with merriment at it! This
way – that way – tottering, capering, panting his lungs up in a
manner most pitiful, while the dead apothecary kept thumping
his back with stiff arms like he was no better than a beast of
burden.

He staggered to the side of the road, for the coach was
coming. Already he could see it, dark and implacable, with the
cold moon gleaming on its carved edges.

He groaned and knelt as if in prayer.

'May you rest in peace, Mister Corbett: and give *me* peace at
last! Good-bye to you – for ever!'

With a roar and a clatter the coach came racketing close. The
horses plunged and shrieked. The huddled coachman shouted;
dragged at the reins.

'Madman! Madman!'

A man – the figure of a man – had toppled drunkenly into
the road: seemed almost to have been pushed. The coach halted.
A white-faced boy came running.

'He's dead! I saw it! He fell in your way! Run down! The coach killed him! I saw it!'

Benjamin Partridge, rid at last of his burden, came panting to the door of the coach.

'An accident!' he cried excitedly. 'No one to blame! I saw it all!'

The coach door opened. Darkness within. Came a cold voice, attended by a snuffle: 'Did you indeed, Benjamin Partridge?'

It was the old man!

5 'Why do you tremble and shudder, Benjamin Partridge? Why do you groan as if in anguish? Why is your face as deathly as the moon?'

The old man spoke softly, but Benjamin was not deceived: softness was not *his* line of business.

'Why are you suddenly silent, Benjamin Partridge?' pursued the old man. 'And why do you spread out your arms as if to hide your dead friend? It *is* Mister Corbett, ain't it?'

He peered sideways at the crumpled corpse that lay behind the boy, its spectacles all awry and shining brokenly.

'Why do you cover your face with your hands and shake as if your soul has taken the ague? Come, young man, answer me.'

'Help me – help me!' whispered Benjamin. 'I can't get

through the gate. I can't bury him. Help me – or I'll be hanged!'

'Very likely, young man. Very likely you will be.'

'But – ' began Benjamin, then stopped. To plead once more he'd never touched his dead master would not be taken amiably by the old man. There'd be a difference of opinion. Benjamin saw it in his bright eyes.

'But what, Benjamin Partridge?'

The old man seemed in no hurry to be gone, even though his coachman shifted impatiently in the cold night air. Once or twice, Benjamin caught his reproachful glance ('Tried to blame me, did you?'), but his face was so shadowed, it was hard to be sure. . .

'But if I'm hanged, I'll not be able to pay you!' cried Benjamin suddenly. (Surely the old man would protect a customer?)

'True enough, young man. And it wouldn't be the first time. You'd be amazed,' he went on, shaking his head as if *he* was amazed, 'how often gentlemen don't pay me. If it's on account of judge and jury, I don't quarrel with it. No one's to blame there. But there's a surprising number who do wild things to avoid payment. Yes, indeed. Hang themselves, shoot themselves, drown themselves, poison themselves, even dash out their brains against the walls of Bedlam! The world's very full of men who fancy it to be more honourable to die than to pay their debts.'

He paused and sighed.

'But you're not one of them, Benjamin Partridge, are you? You've an honest face – even though it's white as bone!'

'No,' muttered Benjamin, sinking into a pit of despair so deep that the moon seemed more than ordinarily remote. 'I'm not one of them.'

Drearily he stared down at the apothecary whose weight was dragging him to the gallows.

'He's only mutton, so to speak,' murmured the old man. 'He can't harm you now. Though his eyes seem to stare, they don't, really. He cannot haunt you, young man. It's not as though he was a ghost.'

'If only he was!' cried Benjamin. 'It's his dead weight that's killing me! I can't go on. My heart's on the burst. Oh, if only he was a ghost!'

'Heart and soul,' the old man reminded him. 'And now the heart proves too weak. What of the soul, Benjamin Partridge? Could your soul carry a ghost? Or would that prove too weak likewise? Consider, young man. Think carefully. Even supposing it was possible, might not a ghost prove too heavy for your soul?'

'*Is* it – is it possible?' whispered Benjamin, spying a faint hope that the old man was melted by pity. A light, easy, effortless phantom would be a wonderful exchange for the terrible corpse.

'All things are possible to the willing soul.'

'Then ... will you – ?'

The old man was overtaken by a fit of sniffing and snuffling that lasted out the passage of a cloud across the moon. Darkness shadowed him till he spoke again.

'I bear you no ill will, young man: not even for trying to lay your victim at my coach door. In my line of business that's common. All I ask is that your soul should be willing.'

'Yes – yes – yes! It is!'

The old man shrugged his shoulders.

'Fetch down my box,' he said to the coachman; and that surly, humped and shadowy figure grunted with displeasure, for the box was large and awkward and cost great efforts to get down.

At last, with a faint jarring, it was set in the road, stout enough and tall enough for the old man to step down upon as he came out of the coach.

With mounting hope, Benjamin watched. To tell the truth, his present circumstance was such that any change would be of a hopeful nature.

The old man fished in his many coats for the key, while the coachman swung his arms vigorously and stamped his feet to keep warm.

The key was found and the old man knelt and unlocked the box. The coachman shivered and swung his arms more vigorously than ever, as if a deeper chill was come into the air.

'I take them wherever I go,' said the old man, lifting the lid and displaying the telltale items from his wall of shelves. 'For they're my only livelihood. My house has been broke into this many a night by – by gentlemen. Can you imagine it? Ah! Right at the top! How fortunate we are!'

He lifted out Mister Corbett's jar and peered at it in the light of the moon. Abruptly, he stood upright and turned to Benjamin. The road must have sloped thereabouts, and the old man been on an eminence, for he now seemed taller than Benjamin – by an inch or more.

'Hold it for me,' he said, and Benjamin took the jar with trembling hands.

'Some folks tie lovers' knots,' he murmured, more to himself than to Benjamin. 'But we tie haters' knots, don't we, young man? Now – now – now it's done!'

He took back the jar with its black ribbon, in which there was now a second knot.

'Look, Benjamin Partridge! Behold your ghost!'

6 Before Benjamin's eyes – his amazed eyes – the apothecary's corpse was on the turn. It had begun to quake and seethe like milk neglected on the hob. Its thin hands seemed to overflow till, where there had been ten fingers, there were now twenty. Likewise the stockinged legs, the old brown breeches, the waistcoat with its stains of oil of camphor and smears of sulphur, the coat (his best), the woollen scarf that he, Benjamin, had given him on his first Christmas – and ever after prayed would choke him – all most subtly and silently boiled over till there was a second Mister Corbett rising like steam unequally from the first.

Extraordinary sight. But not yet done with. Consider the solid Mister Corbett, lying limp and disagreable under the charitable moon. Being empty, his sides shrank in, his face

diminished and the whole of him shuddered into a flabby nothingness – like a shrunken balloon. Then this, too, shrank and came down to a tiny spot of damp that might have been dew.

'No more to him than that?' whispered Benjamin wonderingly to the old man. There was no answer. Benjamin turned. The road was quiet; the coach had gone. So absorbed had he been in the emptying of Mister Corbett, that all sound must have escaped him. Once more he was alone with the perished apothecary.

But the difference – oh, the difference! Beside him now, right beside him, with both feet almost on the ground, stood the apothecary's ghost.

Gone was the gloomy weight, the listless, damning sack of flesh and bone and halted blood. In its place was a Mister Corbett better than new. Not the sharpest eye could have told he was not what he seemed. This fellow could be passed off anywhere as the genuine apothecary.

Down to the same blueness about the chin and the same mole on the side of his nose, it was Mister Corbett. Even Benjamin, though he'd seen every inch rise up uncannily, was momentarily deceived.

'Mister Corbett, sir – ' he said uneasily.

But the ghost did not reply. It stood and stared at the boy in a manner most timidly solemn, like a child on its first day at school.

Now triumph, joy and amazement struggled in Benjamin's breast. His misery was at an end. He felt – yes, he felt in that moment almost pleased to see the luckless man looking so much like himself.

'Mister Corbett!' he cried, and took a pace forward.

The ghost shrank back.

'Mister Corbett!' repeated Benjamin, advancing another step.

The ghost shuddered and put up its imitation arms as if to defend itself.

'Mister Corbett,' said Benjamin for a third time, with much

of the triumph gone from his voice. The ghost's aspect was not encouraging to it: its face expressed terror.

A cold discomfort entered the boy. He thrust his hands into his pockets with an air of defiance.

'What are you staring at, Mister Corbett?'

The terror in the phantom's eyes grew extreme. Mister Corbett was staring at the apprentice who had hated him.

'I – I never touched you, you know,' said Benjamin, and wondered if Mister Corbett had any notion of what had befallen him: if he knew of the house and the black ribbon and the desolate murderers' walk.

Being a spirit, no doubt such knowledge was possible to it. Benjamin shivered. Was it likewise possible that it knew now – for the first time – the scope of the apprentice's hate?

'You brought it on yourself, Mister Corbett. You were as hard as iron,' said Benjamin unhappily.

The ghost's lips moved. Benjamin strained to hear. The voice was all but withered away, having no solid organ at its origin to give it resonance and substance.

'I – am – in – hell . . .'

'No you ain't!' cried Benjamin indignantly, for he was frightened beyond measure at such a striking notion. 'You're on Hampstead Heath, Mister Corbett, as well you must know!'

But the news did not seem to cheer the apothecary's ghost tremendously, and its dread of its murderer did not seem much abated.

'Cold. I am so cold,' it moaned, and plucked at its scarf in that mean and finicky way Mister Corbett had so often plucked at it when he'd been alive.

'It's a cold night, Mister Corbett, so there's nothing unnatural in your feeling it. If – '

He stopped. There was someone coming. A horseman. He whipped round the bend in the road too quick for Benjamin to hide.

'Happy New Year to the pair of you!' shouted the rider, and galloped on.

Benjamin wiped the sweat from his brow.

'The Lord be praised, Mister Corbett! He took you for a living man!'

Sadly, the phantom nodded.

'A living man, Mister Corbett! Think of it! It's only me that knows you're not!'

Filled now with a fine, nervous determination to make the best of his situation, he began to walk back towards the turn-pike.

Then a grim thought struck him. What if the ghost should seek revenge? What if it should accuse him? Was that not the proper office of ghosts?

Several times he turned, longing desperately to ask, 'Would you betray me, Mister Corbett?' But each time the question stuck in his throat and the ghost came on, bent-shouldered, stooping, with that aggravating spying air he'd ever had in life.

'I'm so cold!' it moaned. 'So very cold!' And it continued to spy and peer as if for a warm corner somewhere.

'So it's you again, lad!' said the turnpike keeper, hanging his head out of his window like a battered sign. Then he saw the apothecary's ghost. He stared.

'I thought – ' he began. 'I could have sworn – ' he began again. 'I could have taken my oath that – '

'It turned out that he was only poorly,' said Benjamin, his heart beating furiously. 'And now he's as good as new.'

'I'd have gone bail for his being dead as mutton!' muttered the keeper, shaking his head, while the ghost of Mister Corbett returned his stare in a chilly, melancholy fashion, but spoke not a word.

'Poorly, you said? Now you come to mention it, he does look a bit pale around the chops. And, no offence, it don't improve him any.'

'I'm so cold!' whispered the ghost at last.

'Cold, is he? Not surprised. He ain't dressed over warm. If you've any Christian charity in you, lad (as I hopes is in every mortal soul!), take him into the Spaniard's Inn for a tot of brandy and rum. Half and half, with a sprig of rosemary. That'll put roses in his cheeks! Go on, lad! Be a Christian on this New Year's Eve and warm your freezing friend!'

With all his heart the boy longed to go into the inn, for it was a cheerful place. Its windows shone and there was a smell of roast and onions in the air. But he feared the ghost's accusing finger . . . and cry of 'Murderer!'

'Go on, lad!' urged the keeper, a powerful minder of the world's business.

'Directly! Directly!' cried Benjamin, backing towards the inn and wondering how best he could escape. God knew whether the warmth of a parlour might not give the ghost strength for his damaging cry!

'Would you betray me?' he whispered desperately.

'Betray you?' echoed the apothecary's ghost.

'Accuse me for – for revenge – ?'

'What would I want with revenge? I am in hell and want for – '

But what the phantom wanted for was drowned out by the keeper's impatient cries of 'Hurry, there!' for his kindliness was of an interfering, bullying sort.

'Directly! Directly!' answered Benjamin.

'D'you want help with your friend?'

'No! No!'

He took the spectre's hand. An unpleasant moment, that. Not so much the chill (as of a piece of cold air), but the lack of substance. There was nothing to grasp. His fingers closed in on themselves. Horrible.

He glanced back to see if the keeper had noticed. But for once that nosy fellow had seen nothing.

'A near thing, Mister Corbett,' breathed Benjamin. 'We must be careful. Though you *look* as good as new, there's less to you than meets the eye.'

They had entered the inn yard where tall coaches stood upon the moon-washed cobbles like dark ships becalmed on a silver sea.

Once more Benjamin stopped. The inn beckoned – but he was afraid. He stared back. The keeper was watching them all the way.

'Give you a hand?' he bellowed.

God forbid! Benjamin shook his head and hurried on. Abruptly, a horseboy scuttled from the stables back to the warmth of the inn. He saw the wayfarers – even crossed their path – and briefly waved. He never noticed the uncanny circumstance of two figures approaching with but the sound of a single pair of feet.

This gave Benjamin a touch of confidence, but not very much of it. He glanced sideways at his murdered master, shuffling stoop-shouldered as though his overlong scarf was weighing him down.

'He's bound to betray me,' thought Benjamin gloomily, 'no matter what he says. It's in his nature to betray me.'

But the ghost only shuddered and moaned: 'I'm so cold. Who would have thought hell to be so cold?'

Benjamin Partridge bit his lip till the blood came.

'You're no more in hell than I am, Mister Corbett. And well you must know it! It's a cold night – '

'What's keeping you now, lad?' came the keeper's voice, surly with charitable intent.

A lamp swung gently in the inn's porch. To mark the New Year and good resolutions, someone had polished it and the landlord had bought clean oil. It burned brightly and set off the timber work to advantage.

Benjamin sighed. Sooner or later there was a world to be mingled with. Was not here and now as good a place and time as any?

'You'll not betray me, Mister Corbett? You swear you'll not betray me?'

The ghost looked at him in terror and grief.

'Not I! Not I!'

'All right, Mister Corbett. We'll go into the warm, then.'

They passed under the porch lamp. As they did so, Benjamin's confidence suffered a sharp decline. He had made a detestable discovery. He had seen the lamp through the phantom's head! In the light – in a good light – the apothecary's ghost was transparent!

7 Once within the inn, a thousand fears had invaded
him. Every flicker of flame had terrified him; every
sudden leap of the fire, every glow of a lighted
pipe had given him such dread as only the deepest
shadows could partly dispel.

'For pity's sake, Mister Corbett – keep out of the light!'

Desolately the phantom had returned his frantic looks, as if
unaware of its own infirmity. It hung its head, ashamed of it
knew not what ... and followed its murderer close by the
darkest wall of the candlelit parlour.

It was now half after eleven and the parlour was filled with
travellers and their servants, briefly united in the fellowship of
the hour. The New Year drew nigh and, as the wine flowed

down, good resolutions flowed out, tempered with a rosy whiff of claret.

'Merciful heaven, Mister Corbett! Draw in your shoulder! Oh God! I can see that gentleman's face as plain as day through you!'

The phantom exposed its ugly teeth in a semblance of Mister Corbett's unpleasant smile . . . and drew back against the wall with a pitiful air of shame.

'Thank you, Mister Corbett. That was uncommon obliging of you!'

A dozen times already, he'd had occasion to thank Mister Corbett with such urgent gratitude. Not that the phantom had put itself in the way of discovery, but there were a terrible number of tapers and candles going about the parlour like fireflies, to light extinguished pipes, read letters, admire trifles of lace, even to search for a dropped half-penny.

And each time, Benjamin's heart chilled as he glimpsed the flame through the phantom's substance. It seemed not possible that such an eerie thing had passed unnoticed. Yet neighbours in the room – good, respectable folk – continued to smile at him and murdered Mister Corbett and raise their tankards politely whenever their eyes turned that way. He believed he'd collected enough 'Happy New Years' to see him out at a hundred; and each one provoked more anguish than the last.

With all manner of twistings and turnings and leanings forward, he struggled to cast Mister Corbett into the shadows. An evil moment came when a pair of tankards were passed along the line, one for him and one for the pallid gentleman by his side – 'with the compliments of the House'.

Frantic was his reaching to keep a hold on the second tankard: yet with deep caution lest he poke his arm, hand, tankard and all clean through Mister Corbett. And all the while, that murdered man sat silent by his side, with never a look nor a sound that was not obligingly lifelike; never a reproach on his murderer save in the deathly chill that came from his person and chilled Benjamin's shoulder, arm and thigh.

But what was he doing now, that cold, cold ghost? In fear

and anger, Benjamin suddenly became aware of the phantom's singular behaviour.

First a hand, then a foot, then a hand again it was slyly holding up before the fire. It was charmed by its own transparency! On its face was that self-same look that Benjamin had known so well in life – a deep, absorbed and searching look . . .

'Good God, Mister Corbett! What are you at? You will betray us!'

Guiltily the ghost snatched back its hand and shrank once more into the shade. Piteous were its eyes as it peered at Benjamin, and its thin lips moved unhappily: 'I'll not betray . . . only, give me warmth . . . forgive – '

Gloomily, Benjamin nodded. Unthinking and even childish as the ghost's action had been, he was, after all, lately only human.

Strangeness must still have interested him; company still pleased him; a fire still warmed him. And though he still had Mister Corbett's ugly smile, and Mister Corbett's spying stoop, and Mister Corbett's mean and furtive air, there was a sharp sadness in it all.

'You are a poor soul,' whispered Benjamin impulsively, but the ghost shuddered as if in profound dismay.

'I'll not betray . . . not I!'

'That's uncommon obliging of you, Mister Corbett, sir . . . and I believe you with all my heart.'

Suddenly there was a cry of 'Make way! Make way!' and two servants attended by the landlord and his lady came grandly in with a silver bowl of punch. The room was filled with the hot sweet odours of brandy, spice and the Lord knew what else besides. The Spaniards' punch was a deep secret, and, though many a man had been told it, the cunning spirit fuddled him too much to remember its recipe and carry it home on New Year's Day in the morning.

At once there was a general shifting towards the table in the middle of the parlour – and consequently some space was left before the fire.

The fire. Benjamin saw the phantom stare at it with longing. What with the cheerfulness of the parlour following so hard on his late adventure, and the general obligingness of the ghost, he was moved more deeply than he'd bargained for. He discovered he was not so inhuman as to hate Mister Corbett beyond the grave.

'I'll go stand before the fire, Mister Corbett,' he whispered, 'and then you may stand behind me and warm yourself. No one will see while they're at the punch bowl. Come, sir, move as I move . . . exactly . . . but for mercy's sake, be careful!'

With extraordinary caution, Benjamin stood up and stepped sideways before the fire. He might have been a single figure, though a trifle rheumaticky, for his movements appeared peculiarly stiff and slow.

At last, distinctly – most distinctly – Benjamin heard the phantom sigh and sensed that it rubbed its hands together in Mister Corbett's old oily fashion.

'Are you warm now, Mister Corbett?'

'The fire burns bright,' came the faint reply, and Benjamin smiled benevolently.

In the middle of the room punch was being ladled out in a capacious silver spoon, 'with the compliments of the House'. Much was the noise and entertainment there, and no one spared a glance towards the fire.

'At last, Mister Corbett – a real piece of luck!'

'I make it five minutes more!' suddenly declared a gentleman, consulting his watch.

'Eight,' corrected the landlord. 'It's eight minutes in this house, sir.'

Then someone else – most probably the landlord's lady herself, a respectable, kindly woman – discovered it to be three minutes only to the New Year.

Directly, there was an amiable commotion. Why? Nothing alarming, nothing dreadful – or even disquieting. So why did Benjamin Partridge turn white and glare horribly about him?

'Hands, gents! Hands must be joined!' shouted the landlord, and stretched out his portly arms like a well-fed signpost.

'Come, sirs!' cried his lady above the hubbub, and took one of her husband's hands. 'A circle, now! All join hands for the New Year! You, sir – and you – and you over there! No one must be left out! They say it's bad luck – '

Remorselessly the happy, laughing chain grew as more and more hands were joined. Nearer and nearer the fire it came.

Hands twisting, clutching, grasping, madly dancing, seemed everywhere. Frantically Benjamin stared to his right. A hand as gnarled as a gibbet reached out to complete its chain. He turned to the left. A hand with veins like a hangman's rope reached likewise.

'Got you, young man!' shouted a voice in his ear. His right hand was seized!

'The last link! The last link!' came the cry – for Benjamin had been jerked aside to make way for the last link. Who was it? Why, that pale fellow behind.

'Last link! Last – '

Before the flaming fire, the last link stood pitilessly revealed. A weak link indeed!

Stoop-shouldered, grinning dingily like the Death's Head it was, stood the apothecary's ghost. And the fire was seen burning – right through him!

Hands felt hands tremble and sweat, then grip hard as iron ... then withdraw from each other. Faces grew pale. In the midst of goodwill, in the midst of hope and merriment, what had stalked in?

All began to draw away, shaking with horror at the sight of the phantom: all save the boy who had brought it in. Wretchedly and shamefully, he stood beside murdered Mister Corbett.

'Not I! Not I!' whispered the ghost.

'Murderer!' cried someone harshly and pointed to Benjamin Partridge.

'It was him who brought the ghost! Murderer!'

The cry was taken up in every corner of the room. Even the cheerful, spotty potboy by the punch bowl screamed,

'Murderer!' with his face screwed up in anger, fear and disgust.

'Be gone before the New Year strikes! Get out and take your damnation with you!'

'Outcast! Wicked, hateful outcast! How dared you come among us?'

'Break the glass he drank from!'

'Scour the seat he sat on!'

'Let out the air he breathed!'

'Open the window! Open the door! For he's – '

In the misery of his shame, Benjamin Partridge put his hands to his ears and rushed for the open door. Close on his heels followed the apothecary's ghost, whose chill and despairing aspect repelled all pursuit.

'Not I! Not I!' it moaned. '*I* did not betray!'

8 The clouds were gone and the moon and the stars inherited the black sky. Despairingly the boy and the phantom passed along the whited high road: two figures with but a single shadow.

Where were they going? What home would take them in? Which family would not turn pale with dread and disgust?

The boy walked rapidly; the ghost shuffled desolately in his wake. The distance between them never exceeded a yard, hasten as the boy might. Was it possible he was trying to out-distance the ghost? Maybe ... but his soul was too darkened by the loss of all his hopes to know distinctly where he was going, or why.

He paused. An iron sound filled the air. The bells of St Michael-on-the-Hill were tolling the hour. Midnight. In the distance other bells likewise beat and swung and chimed. The very night seemed a house of bells; and faintly, in between the chimes, came a sound of laughter, cheering and delight. Secure in their parlours, warm and gleaming families rejoiced.

'A happy New Year to you, Mister Corbett,' wept Benjamin, thinking of where those words might have been spoken: in whose company – and by whose fire.

'I did not betray you!' moaned the ghost – to whom all years were, henceforth, alike, and none of them happy. 'Not I.'

'I betrayed *you* – '

'Willingly? Was it *willingly* done?'

Once more those hated words – but, oh, the painful difference! Such a world of pleading and piteous eagerness was there in '*willingly*', that Benjamin could not but nod and reassure the unhappy ghost.

'You were so cold – '

'Hell is cold . . .'

'You were in the Spaniards', sir – on my honour you were!'

But the ghost whispered softly, 'No tavern, tomb, inn or rest for the murdered man. Only a place in his murderer's cold mansion of hate.'

Benjamin shook his head.

'I don't hate you any more, Mister Corbett. I've had my fill of revenge.'

'So where must we go, you and I? Everywhere, I must go with you.'

The boy looked about him at the mild and lovely Heath. Darker still grew his spirit. The prospect before him was dismal in the extreme.

'The woods . . . the fields . . . the dark corners . . . forsaken places . . . the bottom of the sea, maybe, Mister Corbett.'

'If we must. But before that – could I not bid farewell? Could I not see my home once more? Could I not glimpse my children and my wife? A last look to bear away a bright image in the long dark wanderings to come?'

'But ain't you afraid they'll shriek and go distracted at the sight of you, Mister Corbett? For you're a grim object, sir – '

Though he tried to answer evenly and sensibly, his voice shook and broke with a new dismay.

'They'll not see me,' whispered the ghost. 'I'll peer through the parlour window. I'll not be seen. One last glimpse, I implore . . . so brief and to last for . . . so very long.'

'Through the window, then . . . the one at the back?'

Eagerly, the phantom nodded.

'And – and briefly?'

'Briefly!'

'You'll not betray?'

'Not I! Not I!'

It must have been half past midnight when they came to Gospel Oak, for all the houses but one were in darkness. The New Year had been born and safely cried out on the bells. No need to stay up longer. No harm would come to it now.

Benjamin Partridge and the ghost of his master moved cold and silent among the shadows where once they'd walked in the light. They crept towards the one house still awake.

The apothecary's shop stood half-way down the street, upon the right hand side. Candles shone from its windows, front and back. Mrs Corbett and her two children were awaiting the apothecary's return.

'They will be in the parlour,' murmured the apothecary's ghost, 'where I left them before – before – '

'Before what?' asked Benjamin dully.

'Before I left to bring you back,' whispered the ghost – and it was as if the words were torn from his thin substance with pain.

'To bring me back, Mister Corbett?'

'I was sorry to have sent you . . . on such a night. You spoke of pity. I was ashamed. I ran . . . and ran . . . and – '

The phantom's voice trailed away like a piece of drapery, caught in a carriage door, vanishing with a flutter in the speeding night.

It was now that Benjamin Partridge's soul began to groan and crack under the burden of the ghost. Fear, shame and remorse are great weights to endure when there's no remedy.

'Alice!' whispered the ghost sadly. They were by the parlour window, concealed among such shadows as the leafless garden afforded.

Mrs Corbett – a plump, truly plain woman – sat by the fire, looking up from time to time as faint sounds made her think her husband was coming back.

'My love . . . my darling Alice,' sighed the phantom, for this dumpling of a lady was the ghost's dear darling. She was his love, his joy, the fire of his youth and the warmth of his middle life.

Her face was still smooth, though faint shadows crossed it, forerunners of that grief that would soon tear and crumple it when she should know of her husband's end. Unbearable grief – yet grief that would have to be borne.

Burning tears filled Benjamin Partridge's eyes and flowed, scalding, down his cheeks. What had he done? What had he done?

'Come – for pity's sake, come away!'

'My children . . .' whispered the ghost. 'A glimpse of them. A last glimpse – '

Two sons had Mister Corbett: one was eight and the other was rising five. They were no more remarkable to look on than was their mother as they sat by her side awaiting their father's return. They had fair hair and pink faces and sleepy looks about them, even though they'd been promised a New Year's present when their father should return. The older one did not look so much the older – even though he was now the family's head.

'Come away!' breathed Benjamin shakily, for the ghost was very close to the window, helplessly drawn by the sight within. Then –

'For God's sake – no! No!'

The youngest child had looked up. He'd heard something. A twig snapping under Benjamin's foot.

'Go back! Go back, Mister Corbett!'

Too late. The child had seen. Surprise and pleasure shone in his face.

'Papa!' he shouted. 'Look! Papa's in the garden! He's playing a game! He's hiding!'

In vain did their mother cry out that the air was cold and damp, that the hour was late, that their father would come in directly, directly. There was no stopping two such dancing children as they flew out into the garden on the saddest errand in all the world.

Their shouts and their laughter and the glimpses of their shining New Year faces were more terrible to Benjamin than all that had gone before. They were playing hide-and-seek with their father's ghost. Harsh beyond belief was this mockery of their innocence; monstrous beyond measure was this betrayal of their love.

'Papa! Where are you? Come back!'

They saw Benjamin. Shouted: 'Benjamin! Happy New Year! Come and help us catch Papa!'

But the apprentice crouched close to the ground, blinded by his tears.

'Papa!' shrieked the youngest on a dreadful sudden. 'I see you!'

The phantom, caught at last in the child's bright eyes, stood forlorn and still.

'Papa! The present – the present!'

What could the ghost give except terror and freezing cold? But the child was scarcely five and could not know that.

'No! No!' sobbed Benjamin, his proud heart and soul torn to shreds within him. The child was running with outstretched arms – in the way he'd run a thousand times before, and been caught up and swung high by his Papa.

'Papa! Where are you?'

'What have I done? What have I done?' moaned Benjamin Partridge; for the little boy had run and run – and passed through his father like air.

'It was a trick! One of your tricks, Papa – '

Bewildered, the child had stumbled and fallen. Now he stood

up, chilled by he knew not what. Tears came into his eyes.
'Papa . . . where are you? Come back – '

But there was no one there. Despairingly, the apprentice and
the phantom had fled as Mrs Corbett's voice called: 'Tom!
Tom! Come in, dear! The children will take cold!'

Where now was there left to go? The street, only the empty
street. But there was no escape. A coach was coming, casting its
bright yellow light too far and too wide.

The apothecary's shop alone offered sanctuary, bitter though
it was. The shop with its high mahogany counter behind which
Benjamin Partridge and his ghost might crouch in their misery
and their shame and hide, for a little while, from all the world.
For the door to the parlour and beyond was ever closed to Mrs
Corbett and her children. To the last, the apothecary had kept
tenderness out of his daily sight.

But even this refuge was denied. The shop door opened.
Footsteps crossed the floor. Sharp knuckles rapped on the wood
above Benjamin's head.

'Benjamin Partridge! The mixture. You failed to deliver it!'

Benjamin stood up and stared at the New Year's first customer. Now he was tall and thin as a winter's tree and seemed
to fill the shop from floor to ceiling – the terrible old man! His
eyes burned with unnatural fire; but that might have been on
account of his feverish cold.

Benjamin felt in his pockets. Found the undelivered jar. Then
a desperate idea came to him. A frail hope . . .

'Sir . . . we – we only give j-jars in exchange. An empty jar,
sir. Please – have you the – an empty jar? *Please?*'

'Do you mean *this* jar, Benjamin Partridge?' asked the
old man, and held out the fatal jar with its knotted black
ribbon.

From outside came the voice of Mrs Corbett and her children, searching in the garden. Already there was an edge to the
unknowing widow's voice.

'The jar!' pleaded Benjamin. 'The jar!'

'What will you give me now, Benjamin Partridge? I'm not
in business for my health, young man.'

'My heart and soul!' groaned Benjamin, believing at last that he'd done business with the Devil.

'Pooh!' said the old man contemptuously. 'A shifty bargain, that! To offer what ain't yours to give? It seems to me, Benjamin Partridge, that your heart and soul's been pretty heavily mortgaged already.'

'Then take my life, sir,' whispered the crushed apprentice, and prepared to take his last look at the living world which, at that time, consisted in the queer old man and the piteous apothecary's ghost.

'And have you haunt *me*, young man? Not yet – not yet.'

'Then there's no hope for – for them?' He looked towards the door that led to the family's home.

The old man did not answer. A fit of violent snuffles had overtaken him. Then he sneezed three or four times and sprayed the air with the result.

'You're lucky, young man, that I've got such a chill. In my younger days . . . in my younger days things would have been different. But I grow old. And these damp nights – '

Again he sneezed. 'So give me my mixture, Benjamin Partridge, and take back the empty jar. But,' he said, as Benjamin reached out with shaking hands, 'there'll still be something to pay for my trouble, young man. It was to have been a quarter of your life's earnings. Well, in the circumstances, we must make you an allowance, I suppose. Shall we say, a quarter of a week's earnings? Next week's? A quarter. I always work in quarters. Old habits – unlike apothecaries – die hard. That's fair, ain't it?'

'Agreed! Agreed!' cried Benjamin, who'd gladly have settled for a great deal more. 'When shall I pay?'

'You'll see,' said the old man, taking his precious mixture. 'It'll be when you least expect it.'

'The jar!' breathed Benjamin.

'The jar,' smiled the old man – and smashed it on the floor!

'Tom! Tom! What's wrong? Are you in the shop? Are you ill? Answer me!' came Mrs Corbett's voice on the other side of the door.

From long, hard habit, Benjamin reached for a brush and pan to sweep up the sharp fragments of glass.

'Good night, Benjamin Partridge,' murmured the old man mockingly. 'A happy New Year!'

Benjamin moved round to the front of the counter. Mister Corbett's corpse lay at his feet. But where was the apothecary's ghost?

It was rising from behind the counter and smiling meekly, gently, gratefully. Then that poor, fearful, lonely, anxious, obliging phantom laid its hands on Benjamin's breast, nodded as if in confirmation of an interesting fact – and crept back towards its mortal shell. Slowly, slowly it sank, till it and the corpse were one. The fit was perfect. The ghost was gone.

'Tom! Tom! Please answer!' the door handle rattled; the door began to open. . . .

'A happy New Year, Alice!' exclaimed Mister Corbett, rising uncertainly to his feet and rubbing his troubled head!

Loud rejoicing and wild cheerfulness were not in the nature of things for that night. Mrs Corbett and her two children did not – then or ever – know that Mister Corbett had come back from the dead. Instead, their chief pleasure was that Benjamin Partridge had been brought back to drink a health with them all by the family fire.

There was nothing remarkable in Mister Corbett's returning. Indeed, why should there be?

'We should have done this last year,' said Mrs Corbett, much touched by the tears of pleasure that stood in the apprentice's eyes.

'I – I would have,' murmured Mister Corbett, 'but I thought he was so anxious to be off – '

And, though Mister Corbett smiled in his old, old way, his apprentice could not restrain his tears of joy as he clasped his master's hand.

'A happy New Year, Mister Corbett!'

The hand was strong and, thank God, it was warm!

Suddenly he began to wonder if his dark adventure had been

a dream. The thought – the hope, even – took root and grew strong. When Mister Corbett offered, indeed, insisted on taking him home in his own carriage, the hope had become all but a certainty. The Apprentice's Dream. That's what it had been. The Apprentice's Dream of his Master's Ghost. No more than that –

'By the way, Master Partridge,' said Mister Corbett as they rattled towards Kentish Town. 'Did you deliver that mixture?'

'Yes indeed, sir,' said Benjamin uneasily.

'Did the old fellow pay you?'

'I – I forgot to ask, sir. . . . '

Mister Corbett chuckled. 'Never mind, Master Partridge. But I'll have to take it from your wages next week, my boy. It'll be – ' He paused and rubbed his head as if trying to remember something. 'Shall we say a quarter of your next week's wages? We must start the New Year right!'

Benjamin's composure suffered a very sharp set-back, and it was not till they reached Mrs Partridge's – an hour after midnight, but welcome nonetheless – and had sat and drunk healths and 'happy New Years' in the firelight and candle-light, that Benjamin's heart began to beat evenly once more.

'My son is lucky to have you for a master, Mister Corbett,' declared Mrs Partridge cheerfully.

'And I'm lucky to have him for an apprentice,' said Mister Corbett courteously, but with an air of meaning it.

Then Mrs Partridge and Mister Corbett were both surprised and touched by the strength and passion of Benjamin's agreement.

'Lucky?' he cried. 'Lucky? Oh yes, indeed we are!'

For, though he'd studied Mister Corbett as hard as he could, against every manner and source of light, he'd not been able to see through him at all!

But what he had been able to see was a world restored. All its skies, seasons, fruits and joys – all days, nights, friends and pleasant evenings – were back with him once more.

And what he could see also – even then and for ever after, for such things once seen are never forgot – was that obliging, anxious and oddly touching ghost, dwelling in its mansion of flesh: Mister Corbett's soul.

Each time he stared into Mister Corbett's eyes – which he did from time to time when there passed a sharpness between him and his master – he saw that ghost again . . . Then he smiled, and Mister Corbett smiled as he, too, half remembered a strange adventure between them, on New Year's Eve.